Festivals

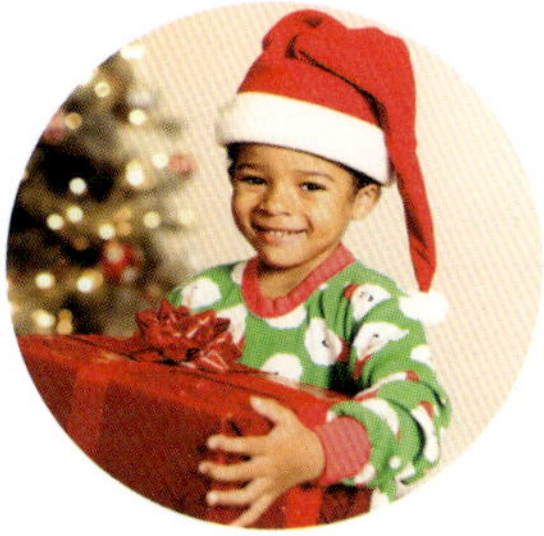

Written by
Stephen Rickard

Ransom

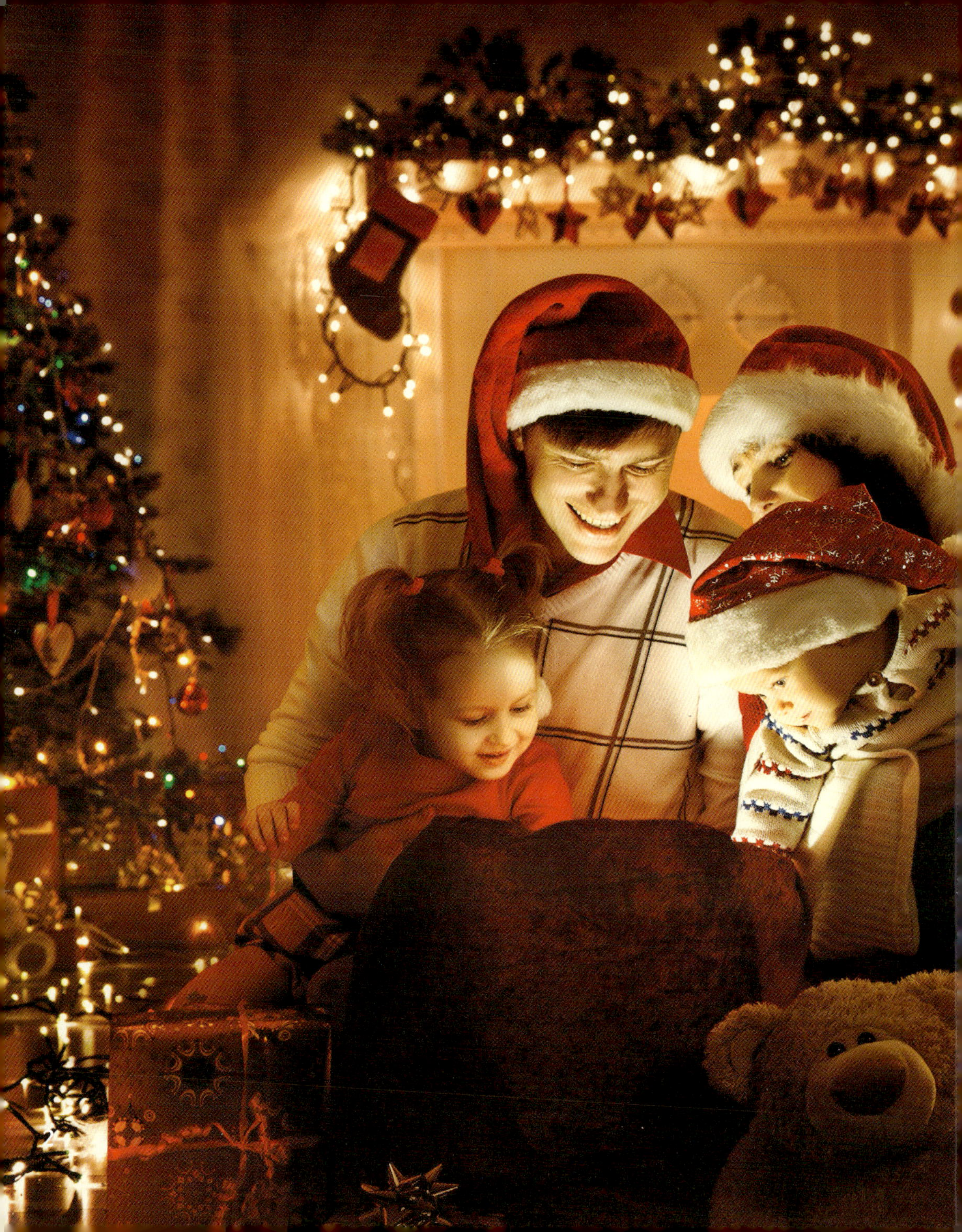

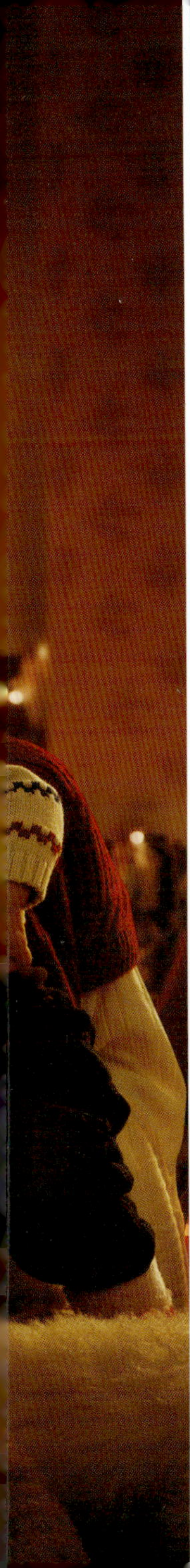

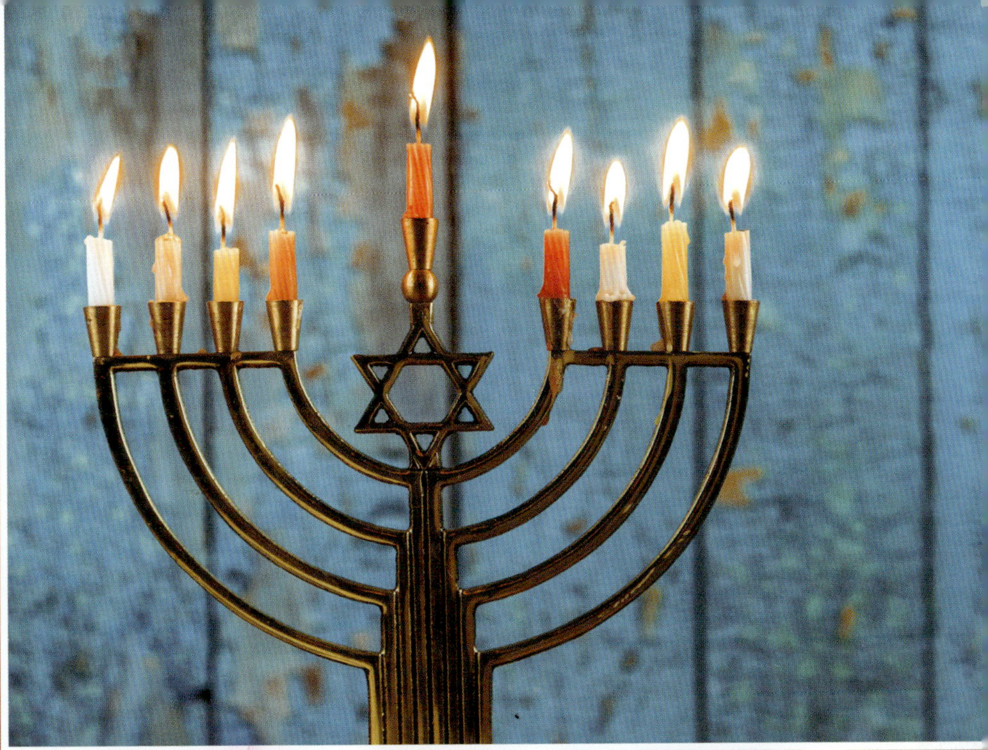

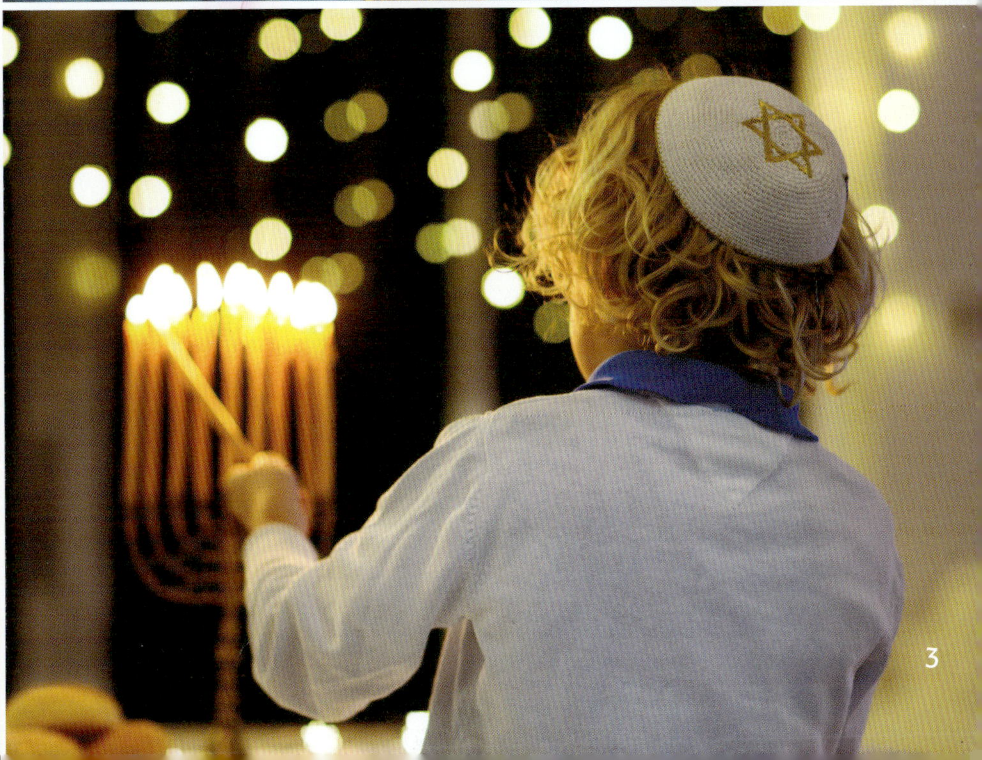

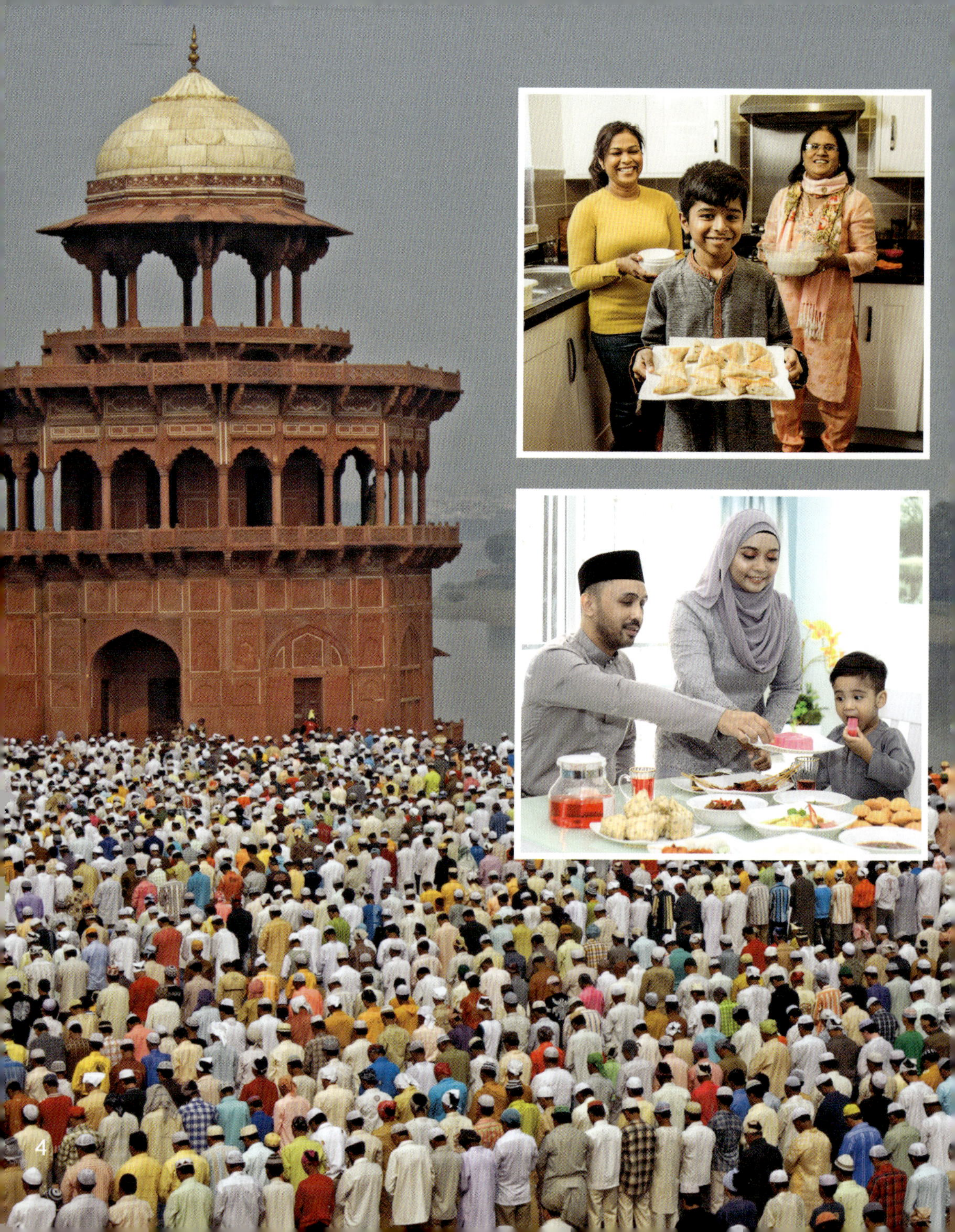

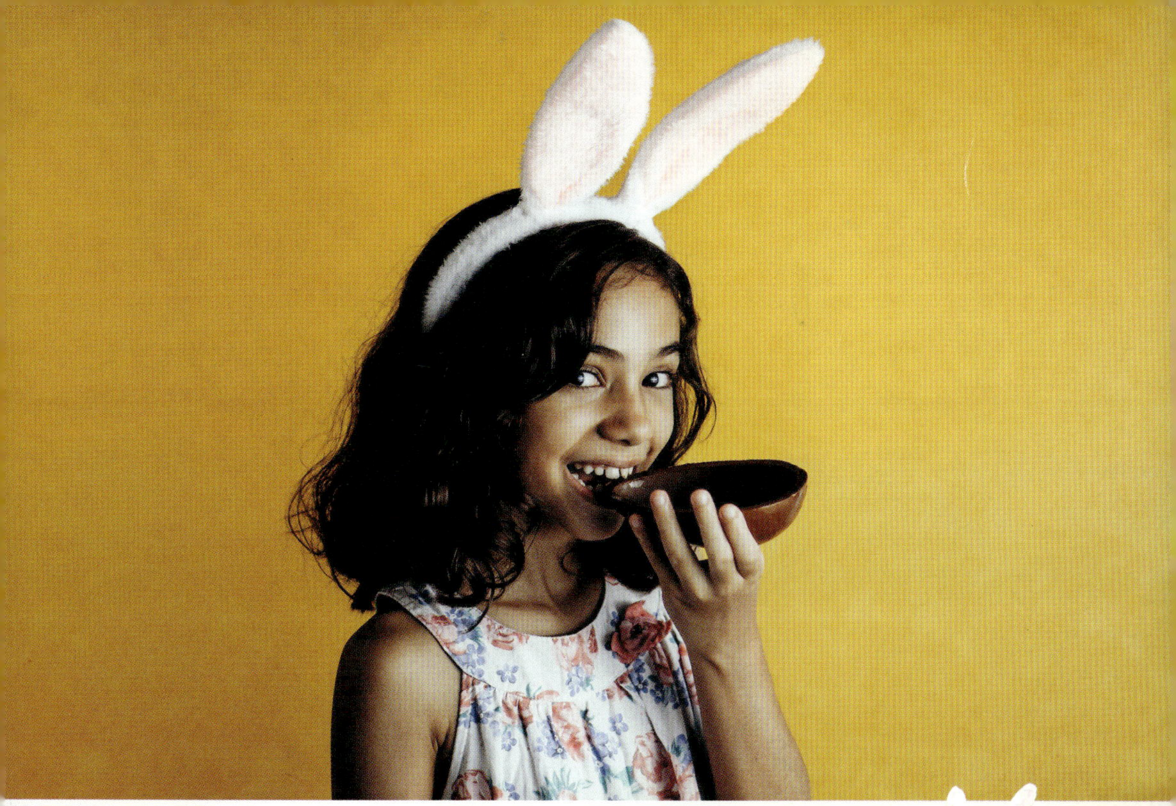

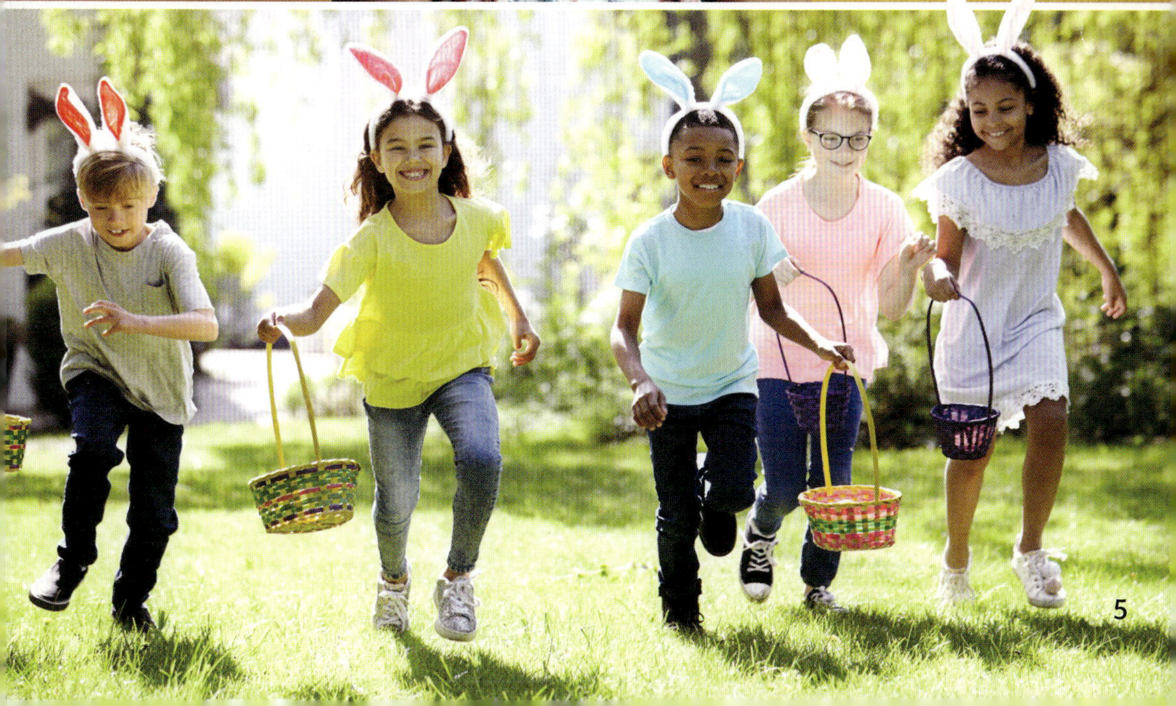

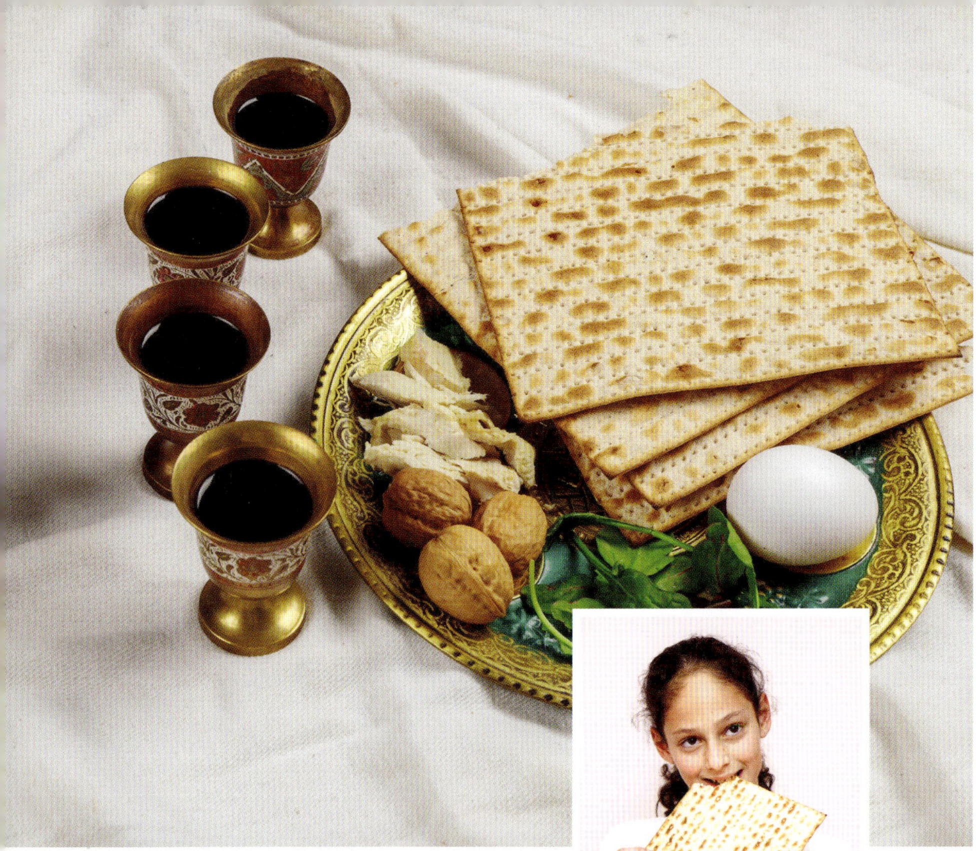

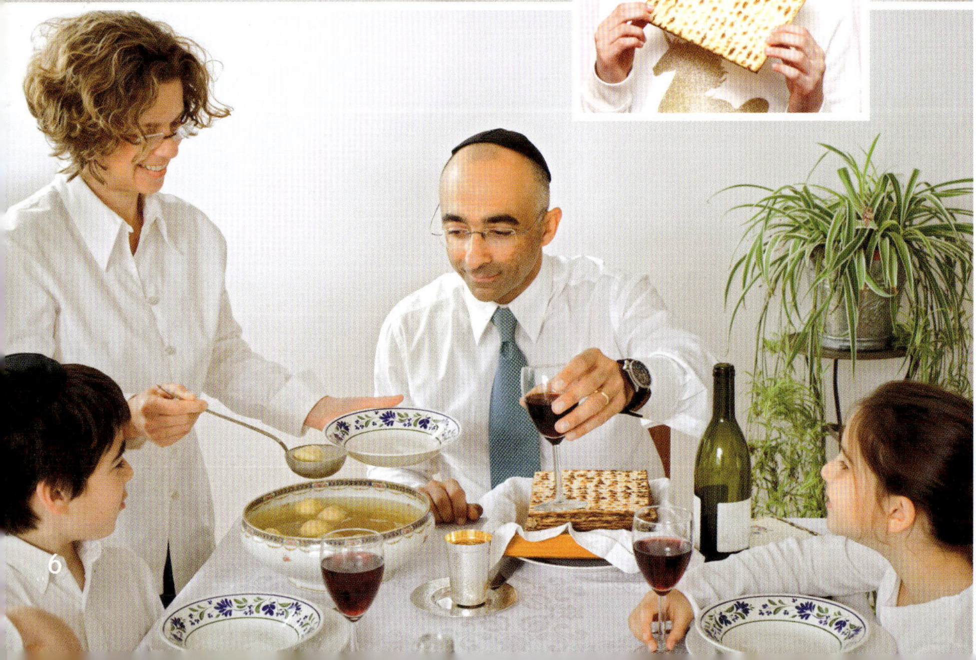

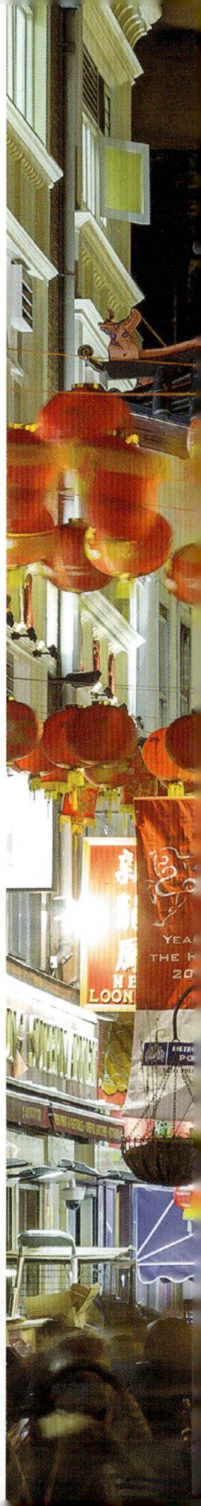

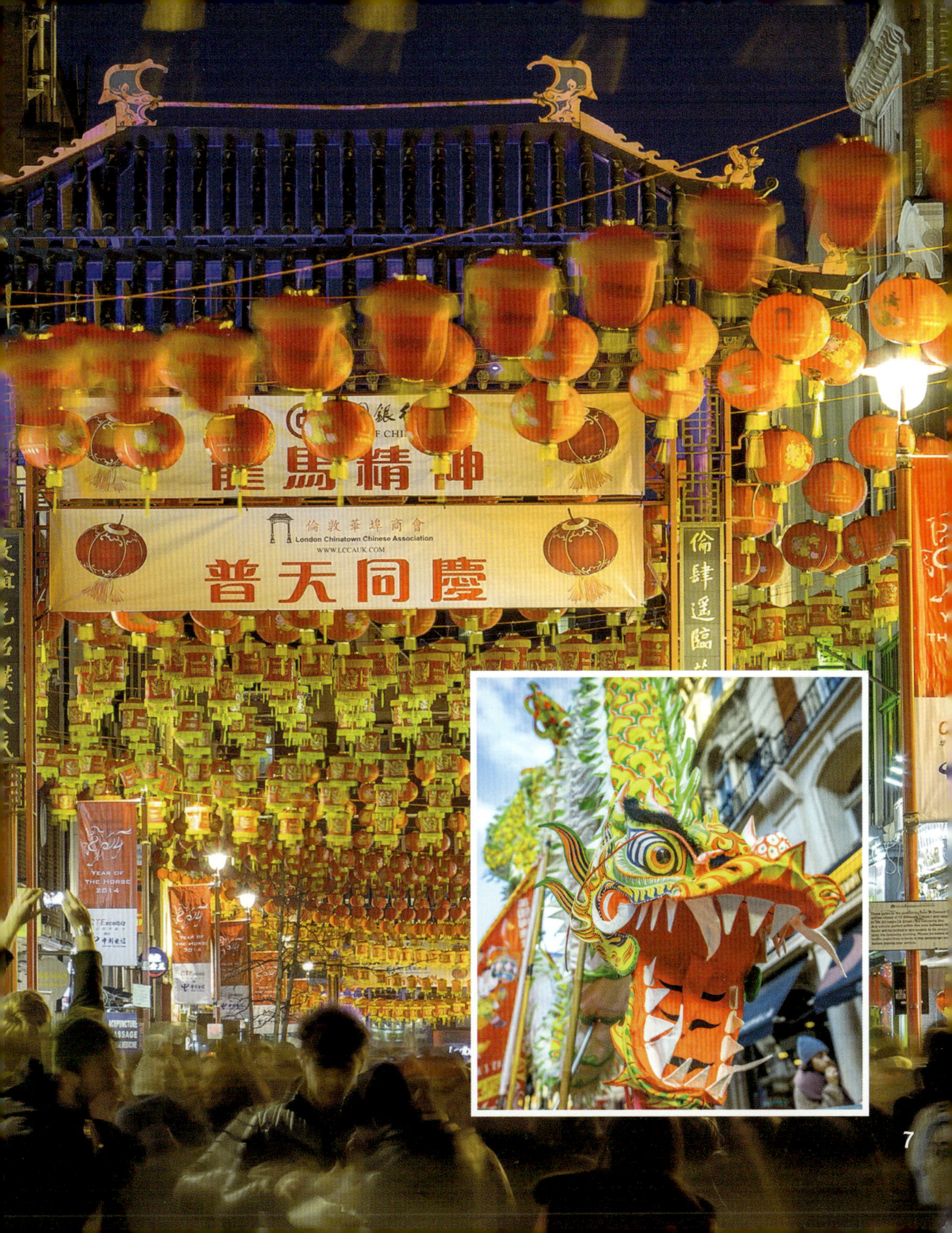
龍馬精神
倫敦華埠商會
London Chinatown Chinese Association
WWW.LCCAUK.COM
普天同慶
YEAR OF THE HORSE 2014

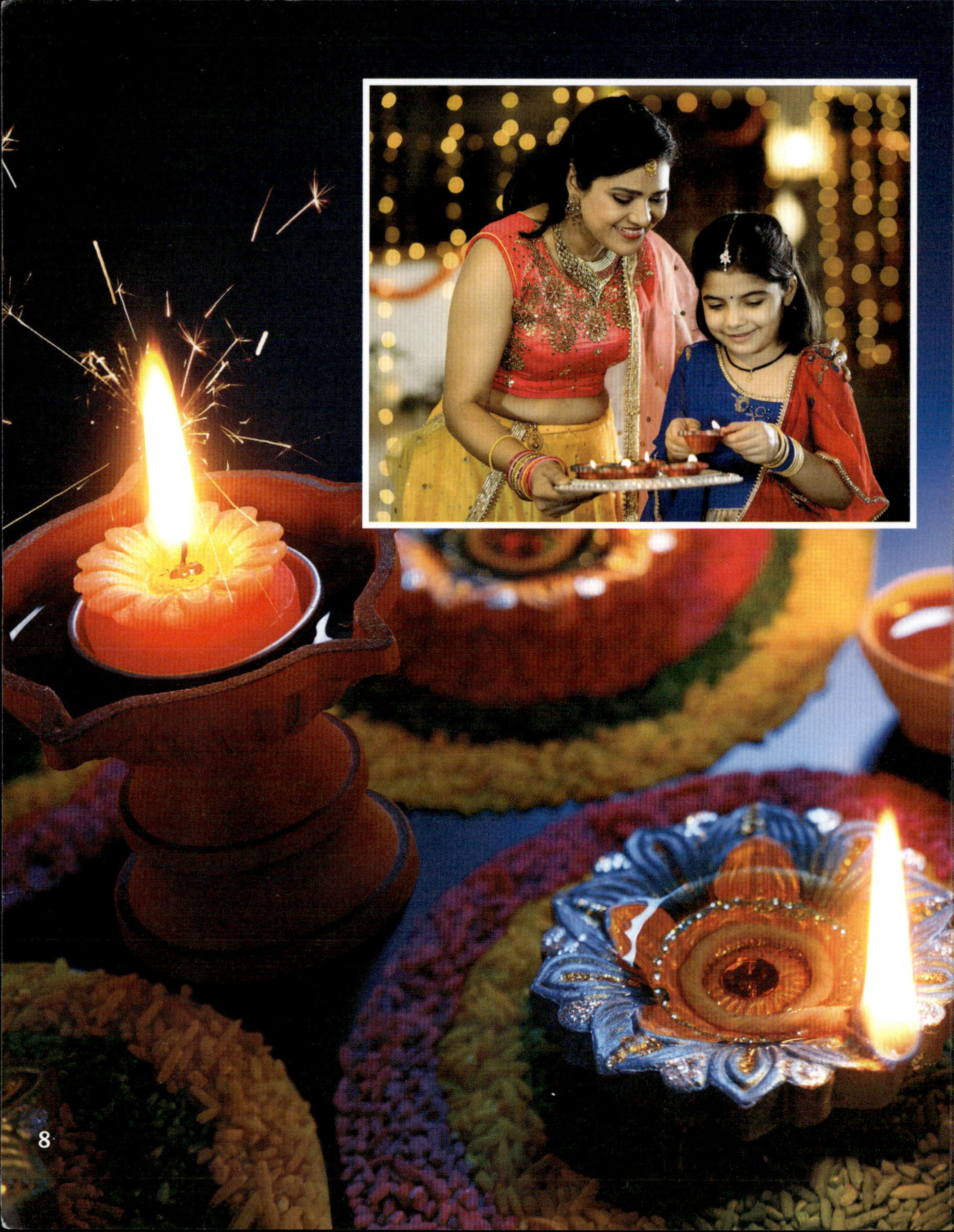